This Little Tiger book belongs to:

Abbie

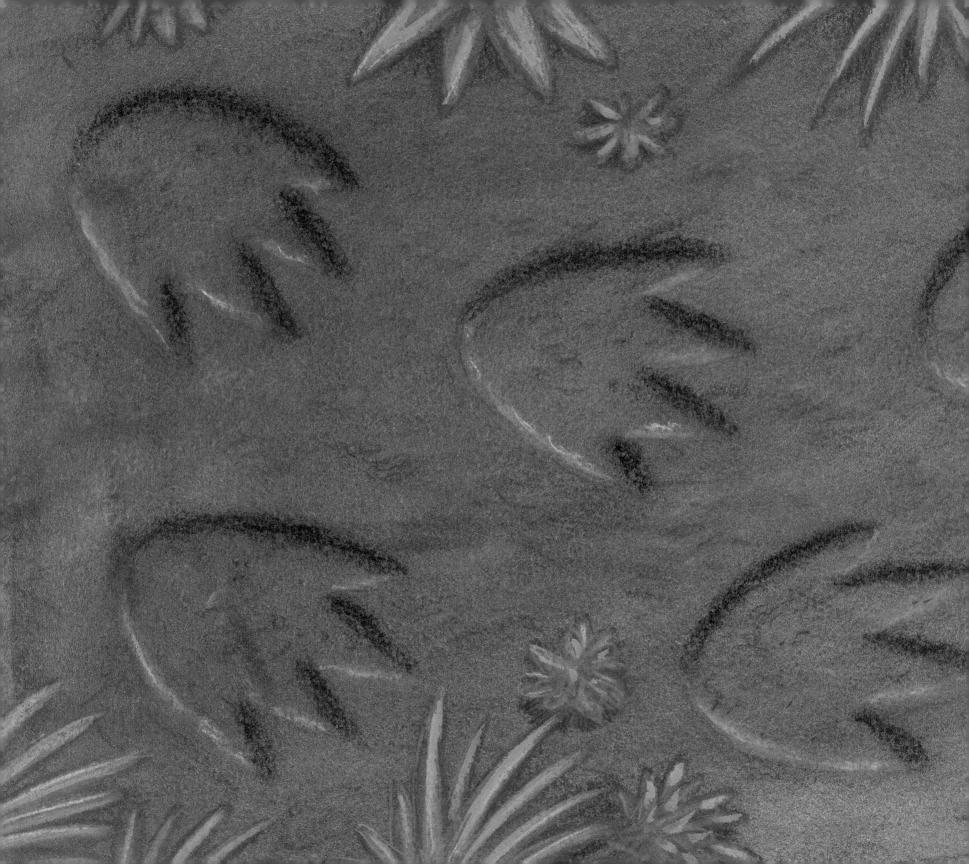

Here comes the

By Kathryn White   Illustrated by Michael Terry

Crocodile

Little Tiger Press • London

It was hot in the deep green jungle when Crocodile leapt from the river. He sniffed and snarled, growled and snapped. The jungle shook and quivered. His long tail whipped as he scuttled along. "I want food to make me strOOOng."

Brown Monkey came
swinging down, to Crocodile's
hungry delight. Crocodile snatched
poor Monkey's tail and Monkey
screeched in fright.

"Oh Crocodile don't you eat me or your
sharp teeth will wobble and drop. You'll go skinny
and sag like a crocodile bag and your great jaws will
dribble and flop. I'm made of sickly chocolate,"
Monkey chattered with glee.

"I knew that," said Crocodile,
creeping away. "You're too
small a snack for me."

Crocodile felt hungrier than ever when he spied through his big beady eyes, two flamingos dancing together: "Now here's a tasty surprise." Crocodile sneaked through the water with a hungry glint in his eye. "Two treats I see, as pink as can be, I'll snatch them before they fly."

The flamingos chuckled
and fluffed, "Why, don't
even take one lick.
We're both made of
sugary candyfloss and
are bound to make
you quite sick.
You'd howl and you'd
yowl and you'd grimace.
You'd swell and you'd
tumble and roll."
"I knew that," said Crocodile,
lying, "I've only come out
for a stroll."

Crocodile marched off defeated with a gurgling
hole in his tummy. He spotted an elephant drinking:
"Elephant dinner, yummy." Into the water he slithered
as swift as a snake in the grass.
And when he got to where Elephant was . . .
he leapt up as quick as a flash.

"Oh Crocodile don't you
eat me or your jaws will
jangle and lock.
For it's quite clear to see you
can't eat me for tea because
I am solid grey rock."
"I knew that," said Crocodile
blushing. "You're a boulder
as big as can be. I'm just out
for a walk, no time to talk
as I'm meeting
a dear friend for tea."

Then Crocodile spied a zebra, grazing lazily
out on the plain. His tummy rumbled,
gurgled and grumbled, hungry for food again.
Crocodile crept through the grass as silent
as he could be.
"I'll sneak up behind him quickly and gobble
up Zebra for tea."

"Oh Crocodile don't you
eat me or you'll turn spotty
and pink from dark green.
You'll splutter and sneeze
and have wobbly knees," said
Zebra polite and serene.
"But you're only a zebra,"
said Crocodile. "You're only
a bright, stripy horse."
"But my black stripes are very
hot pepper and my white
stripes are salt, of course."

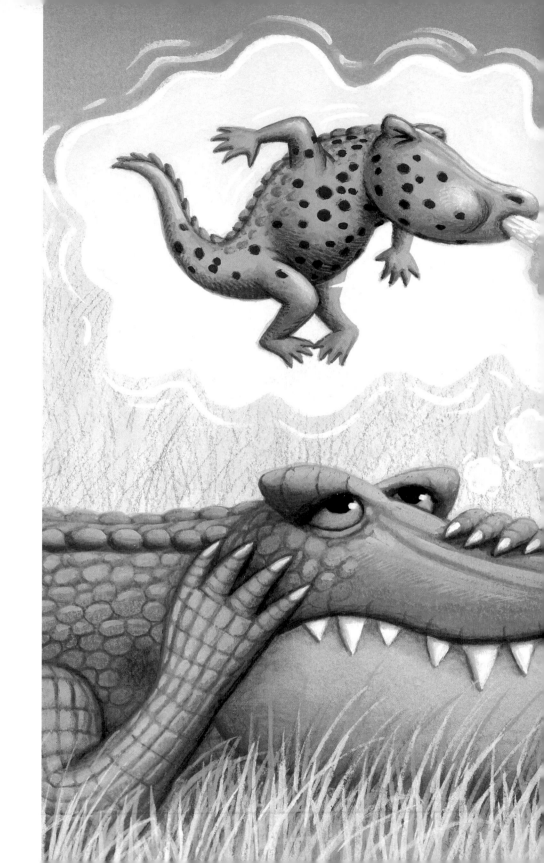

"Oh boo hoo!" yowled Crocodile, shedding big tears. "I feel like I haven't eaten in years." He blubbered and bawled and wallowed and squalled. He rolled on his back, which looked very funny, then wailed and hollered, "I want my mummy!"

"Don't worry," said
kindly young Zebra,
"you can share all
my grass with me."
The two pink flamingos
brought treats to share,
with Monkey's
bananas for tea.
"And I've brought some
clear, cool water," said
Elephant trumping a spray.
And Crocodile grinned
with his big sharp teeth
and said, "What a
wonderful day!"

It was hot in the deep green jungle
as the animals played by a tree, when
Tiger leapt out from behind them,
growling, "I am ready for tea!"

For Charlie, my inspiration
~KW

To my son, Jamie,
my little crocodile
~MT

LITTLE TIGER PRESS
An imprint of Magi Publications
1 The Coda Centre, 189 Munster Road, London SW6 6AW
www.littletigerpress.com

First published in Great Britain 2004
This edition published 2004
Text copyright © Kathryn White 2004
Illustrations copyright © Michael Terry 2004
Kathryn White and Michael Terry have asserted their rights
to be identified as the author and illustrator of this work
under the Copyright, Designs and Patents Act, 1988
All rights reserved
ISBN 1 85430 979 X
A CIP catalogue record for this book
is available from the British Library
Printed in Spain by Grafo S.A.
5 7 9 10 8 6

Snap up a book from Little Tiger Press

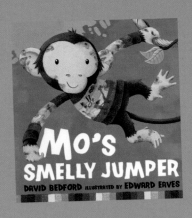

QUIET!
Paul Bright
illustrated by
Guy Parker-Rees

MO'S SMELLY JUMPER
DAVID BEDFORD ILLUSTRATED BY EDWARD EAVES

Night-Night, Poppy!
written by Claire Freedman
illustrated by Jane Massey

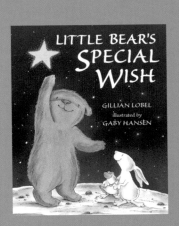

LITTLE BEAR'S SPECIAL WISH
GILLIAN LOBEL
illustrated by
GABY HANSEN

Yummy Yummy Food for my Tummy!
Sam Lloyd
Jack Tickle

3, 2, 1 Bedtime
by Sam Lloyd
Illustrated by Ben Cort

For information regarding any of
the above titles or for our catalogue,
please contact us: Little Tiger Press,
1 The Coda Centre, 189 Munster Road,
London SW6 6AW
Tel: 020 7385 6333 · Fax: 020 7385 7333
E-mail: info@littletiger.co.uk
www.littletigerpress.com